The Legend of Sidora

Further titles from LinguaBooks

Narrowboat Blues
In A Strange Land
A Busker on Bow Street
Lost Dreams
The Farmer's Son
The Seasonal Visitor

The Legend of Sidora

Spirit of Canals and Goddess of Inland Waterways

As curated and annotated by Dr Raymond J Haggart

Maurice Claypole

LinguaBooks
www.linguabooks.com

Paperback edition: ISBN 978-1-911369-38-7
eBook edition: ISBN 978-1-911369-37-0

Special edition

Editor: Ann Claypole
Proofreader: Marie-Christin Strobel

Copyright © 2021 LinguaBooks

A CIP catalogue record for this book is available from the British Library.

LinguaBooks
Elsie Whiteley Innovation Centre
Hopwood Lane
Halifax HX1 5ER
www.linguabooks.com

*Origins are by their nature shrouded in mystery
but what would life be without the unknown?*

Bhavaraju S Rangarajan

Editor's note

At the time of writing, the 55-foot narrowboat, Sidora, based on the Staffordshire and Worcestershire Canal is the only vessel known to bear the name of the Spirit of Canals and Goddess of Inland Waterways.

Foreword

When sorting through my late uncle's papers and selecting manuscripts for publication, I was unable to trace the precise origins of the *Ballad of Chevron and Sidora* or the legend on which it is based. Clearly, parallels may be found in various mythologies throughout the ages, but the unique context of this story and its focus on the still waters of man-made canals and navigations set it apart from the more familiar stories of sirens, mermaids, sea sprites and marine deities. In releasing these documents, I hope I have made a small contribution to the culture of the inland waterways and aroused further interest in aquatic lore.

Dr Raymond J Haggart

Part One

The Ballad of Chevron and Sidora

If in these still waters
you catch a fleeting glimpse
of two young lovers in sweet embrace
learn now who they are and of their fate

A dashing water sprite is Chevron
gossamer skin as sleek as moonlight
lithe and agile as any eel
a toying smile conceals his strength

An aqueous waif Sidora is
dainty of form and swift as the spray
eyes gleaming in watery light
as befits a child of the deep
born of a gushing torrent of love
a mystical union in swirling seas
that took place aeons ago
a river nymph, daughter to the god of the rivers
and the goddess of the lakes,
Sautun and Chalyra, her disaffected parents
supreme rulers of the sweetest of waters

Chevron, too, of noble birth,
crown prince of underwater life
spirit of the teeming creatures that swim and crawl
fashioned so long ago and yet forever young
Sidora his element, he her life
Sworn to be true, to never part
they share the ardour of their youth
swirling in each other's arms

Unburdened by earthly woes
they delve in joyful harmony
safe in the womb of their watery world
of air and land they know not
never fear the raging wind above
never tread on the treacherous shore

But sweet temptation draws Chevron's heart
toward the surface and closer to doom
head above water he beholds
a wondrous world of green and light
of exotic sounds and a wafting breeze
of scents unknown and sights untold
to the land he is drawn and declares it safe:

Come, follow, come see these new delights

The fateful words entice his beloved
but Sidora, fearful, yet holds back
till his assurance and the knowledge of his love
win her over and she obeys

Half risen from the stream
the demi-paradise holds her gaze
until the shattering hand
of fate smites from the unknown.
a menace, lurking, had let Chevron pass,
biding its time, hoping for a sweeter treat
a chimera of earth and air
a creature not of the water,
slithering from the land unseen
crushes Sidora with its fearsome grasp
strangling her breath yet in her throat

A gurgling scream sends crashing waves
as the life force fades from Sidora's face

11

Chevron, stricken with remorse, cries out in pain:

Hear me, gods and spirits, let my folly not be her doom,
take me, but let Sidora live!
for without her, I shall surely perish.
without my love, there can be for me no life

Far and wide his penitent wail resounds
till from the water deep
speaking through the mists of time
echoing through seas and oceans and rivers
and reaching him even as he laments
a sombre tone as old as the seas replies:

For what you have done,
you must bear the pain
but death is not your fate

By venturing beyond our flowing realm
you have brought sadness and agony into our world.
an eternal wrong earns eternal redress
mere nothingness is no recompense;
enduring loss your penance shall be

To live without love, without hope
sequestered in a life of endless forfeit
with no-one by your side,
alone in the desolation of your own making;
your endless penance it shall be
to live on as Sidora fades beyond the light

At this Chevron's tumult of agony and remorse
is imbued with wrath at this merciless judgement

How can this be just – to punish with death
a joyful spirit whose only fault was to follow
my impetuous lead?

Thus Chevron pleads his case to no avail
relentless, Sautun yields not, but remains
firm is his resolve to extract dire retribution

But so loud is Chevron's lament, that another
awakes from the deep
torn between her husband's ire and the
love of her fading daughter,
Chalyra, not for love of Chevron, but for
the survival of sweet Sidora,
quenches the fury of her lord and equal
And to her husband gently proposes:

Let Sidora retain her life, but at a price.
Chevron's folly cannot be without forfeit.
he has no place in our teeming depths,
but let our daughter swim free

And yet, the god does not relent:

But she, too, was guilty of deserting our realm
if she lives, she too must suffer.
and if she should not fade, where shall be the penance
of knavish Chevron?

Sweet lord, says Chalyra, *hear my word:*
many aeons have we been parted
for you, too, in former times, were rash
and I have shunned you as you would deny Sidora's love.
let me pronounce the judgement in this case
and I will return to your watery fold
On one condition, says the lord of the waves,
that your judgement be fair and that I
decree it to be so.
for 'tis not forgiveness that is here required
but a righteous punishment

13

Thus agreed, and each convinced to have their way,
Chevron is called to hear his fate from Chalyra's lips:

It shall be as you wish; Sidora shall live
but for her to return to the flowing current of life
you must remain in still waters,
the flow of your life energy passing to her
so neither of you shall enjoy both current and depth
mighty barriers shall be erected so that
you both may live, but be together
only when the gushing flow of mighty water
rushes through the stillness of the yielding gates

And by your own hand shall this be accomplished
for it is in your gift as prince of the waters
to transfer your energy to Sidora, so that she may cascade
whilst in stagnant domains you reside
and thus ye both shall live, and love shall not be
eternally banished nor forever present
but your time shall ever ebb and flow, the pulse of your life
to be marked by endless parting and reunion
and in the greater balance, the love you cannot share
will live on between my husband and me

And addressing now her words to her estranged spouse,
Chalyra sought his promised assent.
Sautun, my lord, is such pronouncement just?
And Sautun saw that indeed it was.
his anger quelled, and at the joy of this unexpected reward,
embraced his re-won goddess and acquiesced:

Between strong walls the miscreant shall be entrapped.
Chevron shall live, but be imprisoned;
Sidora shall live, but be forever flowing

As the ancient deities rejoiced in new union,
Chevron's piercing wail reverberated through
the flowing world
As he passed his power of movement on to Sidora,
filling her with new life as once again her eyes sparkled
and caught a fleeting glimpse of her lover as the current
tore her away, for he could no longer move with her and
she could not remain still

Thus was born for Chevron and Sidora a new life,
a new cycle of meeting and parting, of loving and leaving
life within death and death within life,
eternally apart and eternally together

If in these still waters
you catch a fleeting glimpse
of two young lovers in sweet embrace
think on their temptation and of their fate

Part Two

Origins and legend

Sidora was born of the union of Sautun and Chalyra, the god and goddess of freshwater life. Far from the rage of Neptune, long estranged from the intrigues of Undine and Carphal, Sautun and Chalyra reigned supreme in the inland waterways, the rivers and lakes of pure, salt-free waters, teeming with life, piscine and mammalian, reptilian and amphibian life. After presiding over their freshwater realm for an age of ages, Sautun became restless and in a fit of temper tore away to plunge into the depths of the brine but was reposted by an army of water-horses driven on by Poseidon himself. For his betrayal of their inland domain, Chalyra henceforth shunned Sautun's attentions until they were reconciled as a result of their intervention in the trial of Chevron. In one version of the legend, Sautun is god of rain and flood and accordingly only meets Chalyra when the heavens open in times of crisis. This, too, is later mirrored in the fate Chevron and Sidora.

In a shorter poem, *The Temptation of Sidora*, now thought to be lost, it is the forest or the forest air that crushes, or more accurately, stifles the sea-creature Sidora, whereas her lover, previously an amphibian, loses his ability to survive in water and becomes a creature of the land.

The chimera of the full legend is the entrapment of free-flowing waters brought about by mankind through the creation of artificial waterways, and the sacrifice of Chevron is his personal entrapment between the arrow-shaped locks that restrict, then release the flow of life, precious water gushing into each lock, whirling and eddying in joyous delight for such a brief moment before hastening out again through the lower gates.[1] In this brief moment, Chevron, forever entrapped between the towering lock gates, receives his lover as Sidora rushes headlong into his arms, their embrace both fleeting and violent, brief but ecstatic, a joyous exhilarating moment of unison before the current tears them apart, Sidora's kiss lingering on Chevron's lips, her outstretched arm waving a poignant goodbye as she is dragged by the torrent into the next pound – goodbye but not farewell, because they will meet again at each recurrence in and endless cycle of filling and emptying of replenishing and depleting, lovers destined to be united and torn apart in an endless sequence of flowing energy, fluid life and boundless love.[2]

---

[1] In one version of the legend, Sautun condemns Chevron to be entrapped "in a silent fortress" or "between vast portals". This does indeed seem to indicate the function of river barriers developed in antiquity and canal locks as we know them today.

[2] A moralising aspect is indicated in additional final lines found on a single manuscript of the ballad, but these are deemed to have been added in Victorian times: "Consider their origins, temptation and fate / And heed the warning therein construed / To retain the borders of thy estate / and venture not from your element true".

Part Three

Uremariak

Numerous legends throughout the ages trace the joy and agony of lovers fated to meet and doomed to be torn apart by the forces of nature, the whims of mankind or the vengeance of the gods. As such, the legend of Sidora is a depiction of the human condition, and the agony of Chevron expresses man's inquisitive nature which is paradoxically both life-affirming and self-destructive. The ebb and flow of the spiritual life force is a motif found across all cultures, and the desire to glimpse beyond one's own horizons transcends the limitations of time, distance and language. It is a fundamental drive portrayed and perpetuated since the earliest songs and ballads and familiar to scholars, storytellers and dreamers in all corners of the earth.

The birth of Sidora is also referenced in the chronicle "Uremariak", perhaps best rendered in modern English as "Water Must Flow". This version of the legend ascribes an alternative genesis to Princess Sidora, the meme of still waters, an indication maybe of how mankind's perception of the elements has changed over time. The following would appear to be the only extant version of this narrative.

Water Must Flow

Among the aqualife, flowing free, a restless sylph meandering through the rials of Argalon, Claryph swims with the finned and finless, blessed by the strong and blessing the weak, her crystal laughter spreading joy throughout her eddying world.

At play in the sparkling waters of Duwanin, she senses a fresh current, an enticing new life force drawing her ever forwards with the vast, vibrant stream, then branching off into a new, unexplored stretch of aqualine; happily, she joins the flow.

A further joyous rush of water gushes into it, teeming down the hillside from the lofty terrain above

But not now the broad watercourse she has left, but a narrowing channel, too shallow to bear the teeming life from the rials, too hard at its depths for the aquaphile flora to find home and sustenance.

And yet the water flows. Then suddenly stops. A solid edifice holds all at bay, a gigantic portal holding back the force of life. In panic, Claryph turns around, riding what remains of the current, flowing upstream But, here, too a great structure, made of hardy arboreal material, blocks her path.

Thrashing frantically about in panic-stricken whorls, the spirit of the free-flowing water feels her life force ebbing away as the trapped waters slow to a residual current, kept alive only by the gushing jet rushing through the thankfully ill-fitting chevrons of two mighty stop gates

A scream such as never before has been emitted from the waters of Argalon tears through the skies, a cry for help that reaches beyond the land of Duwanin, through the void into the swirling realm of Nestor, where it is heard and heeded.

23

In response, a thunderous crack, a strike of brilliant light and from the heaven, joyous water pounds down, covering field, plain and tretalis and bringing life once again to the carahtal, the trapped water of Claryph's deadly prison

In this gorgeous flood, a joyous unison as Claryph is embraced by the relentless Precipitas, giving herself gladly to his strength and drinking in his torrential life force.

Once again, the waters eddy and whirl, streaming over the prison walls, filling the downstream pool and over and through the subsequent sharaptals, across the plain and back to the teeming expanse of mighty Duwanin. Claryph rides the waves, surges with the surf and is free, her laughter filling the air, mingling with the rain and caressing its watery fingers as the downpour recedes and Precipitas returns to the clouds.

As the storm abates, order is restored; Claryph once again is free to roam and weaves happily through her underwater world, but wiser now, she will never again venture into the still waters of the narrow carahatals, never again be caught in Sharap's harsh prison.

But in the still waters, something stirs, for of the union of Claryph and Precip is born a new child spirit, the meme of still waters, gentle and playful at first, barely stirring but and soon to grow with the vast proliferation of carahtals into a graceful lady, powerful in her own right, Princess Sidora, goddess of canals and navigations, supreme spirit of the inland waterways.

෨෮-෬

NOTES

rial – river
Argalon – homeland (England)
Duwanin – name of river that fed the first ever canal
aqualine – water, waterway
placid – a body of still water, a lake.
Precip, Precipitas – god of rain and snow
carahtal (also karahtal, karahtalis) – canal
sharaptal – lock, prison
tretalis – trodden path, towpath

Appendix
Britain's Inland Waterways

The waterways referred to in the notes to these manuscripts and by association in the manuscripts themselves are the navigable rivers and canals of the United Kingdom. Since readers in other countries may not be familiar with the history, traditions and current status of these important waterways, it seems appropriate to include a brief description of them and of the important part they continue to play in the cultural life of the nation and more specifically in the leisure industry.

In terms of rivers, Britain's longest waterway is the River Severn, running 220 miles from Wales to Bristol, England, where it enters the Atlantic Ocean. The Trent and Mersey rivers drain large areas of central England, whereas the Thames, perhaps the most familiar river to visitors from abroad, is the deepest river in the United Kingdom and flows through Oxford and London into the North Sea.

Of greater significance in terms of the legend, however, are the artificial waterways which by their very function and definition, consist of still waters maintained at a constant depth and carefully controlled to preserve precious water and maintain navigability.

Britain's canals enjoy a long and colourful history with the earliest canals being built to carry agricultural produce, usually at the instigation of aristocratic landowners. The golden age of canals, however, began some 300 years ago and was driven by the need of an increasingly industrialised society to transport heavy materials over great distances as cheaply and efficiently as possible. In the first half of the eighteenth century, many river navigations were created, especially in the industrial north of England and these were followed by brand-new watercourses which used a complicated arrangement of locks and reservoirs to enable horse-drawn craft to climb great heights.

Early projects linked inland towns and factories to seaports and provided a low-cost method of transport for carrying coal, building materials and other heavy goods from their point of origin to the centres of production. When the Bridgewater Canal was opened in 1763, the cost of coal at the point of use was effectively halved overnight.

The construction of the canals presented numerous engineering challenges and many of the ingenious systems developed by prominent canal engineers such as James Brindley and Thomas Telford are still in existence today.

Notable landmarks and feats of engineering dating from the golden age of canals are the three-thousand yard long Harecastle Tunnel and the Anderton Lift on the Trent and Mersey, the Barton Swing Aqueduct on the Bridgewater and the Pontcysyllte Aqueduct carrying the Langollen Canal at a height of 120 feet across the River Dee.

Also clearly in evidence on the canals are the locks used to raise and lower boats as they navigate the often hilly terrain of the British landscape. With their heavy gates, robust ironwork and chevron-like pairs of balance beams, they dominate many stretches of the canalscape, often so close together that they form a 'flight' or even a 'staircase', whereby the lower gate of each upper lock forms the upper gate of the lock below. Formerly operated by full-time lockkeepers, it now generally falls to the boat-owners themselves to open and close the locks as they pass through.

In addition to providing a method of transport, the industrial canals were vital source of employment and crucial to the livelihood of many specialised and semi-skilled occupations, from lock keepers, stable hands and boat operators to the leggers who would transport boats through the narrow tunnels by lying on a narrow plank hanging off the side of the boat and walking along the side of the tunnel, weaving their feet over one another and thereby propelling the vessel through the damp dark tunnel, hazardous and claustrophobic work indeed.

With the advent of the railways, however, horse-drawn cargo transport on the canals began to decline in the middle of the nineteenth century, although many canals remained successful and continued to carry goods on motorised vessels well into the twentieth century. The end of industrial-scale canal transport came in the winter of 1963/4 when freezing conditions halted all goods transport on the navigations, effectively transferring most of the business to road and rail, a situation from which the canal carrying companies never recovered.

Consequently, the canal network was largely abandoned and fell further into decline, but by then another force was at work.

Just a few years before the nationalisation of the canal system in 1948, an engineer and, as it turned out, adventurer sowed the seeds for what was to become a key leisure activity within the United Kingdom and ultimately led to the preservation and restoration of much the canal network. In his book, 'Narrow Boat', L. T. C. Rolt described how, motivated by nostalgia for the colourful life of canal people, he restored a former working boat and set out on a journey of discovery. His account of the unspoilt charm of the waterways and way of life of a past era struck a chord in many people and led directly to the founding of the Inland Waterways Association (IWA), an organisation dedicated to restoring the canals to their former glory and promoting their use for leisure purposes.

Although it was a long and painstaking undertaking carried out mainly by unpaid volunteers and enthusiasts, restoration work began on many parts of the canal network and as a result, boaters and other leisure-seekers can enjoy over 2,000 miles of navigable inland waterways offering a wealth of culture, entertainment and heritage events – as well as hire boats, museums and canalside pubs.

Britain's canal network is currently managed and maintained by The Canal & River Trust, a charity formed in 2012 to take over the responsibilities of the former state-owned British Waterways, whilst the Inland Waterways Association, the organisation co-founded by L. T. C. Rolt in 1946 and also a registered charity, continues to play a significant role in the conservation, maintenance and development of the canals and river navigations of the United Kingdom.

Largely as a result of these efforts, the twenty-first century sees the number of boat owners constantly increasing, many choosing to cruise for a few weeks or months each year and others living permanently afloat. Although canal boats, like other vehicles and vessels, come in all shapes and sizes, there is one type of boat which clearly stands out, the narrowboat. With a beam of about seven feet, a narrowboat is about half the width of (and not to be confused with) a barge, and yet narrowboats can be quite roomy and, contrary to a common misconception, offer adequate ceiling height throughout the living area.

Many narrowboats have been lovingly restored or specifically constructed to echo the colourful tradition of canal life and are suitably adorned with the names of carrying companies and the ubiquitous motifs of roses and castles. In earlier times, images of roses and castles adorned almost every part of a narrowboat from fixtures and fittings to harnesses, doors and lamps. Sadly, many of the traditional crafts of the early narrowboat owners have been lost and with them much of the folk tradition which would once have been familiar to those who plied their trade on the waterways. Although there are obvious links with the travelling people, Romany culture and the elaborately painted caravans of pre-industrial traders, the origins of their art, and doubtless many of their stories and folk tales, have been lost. In this, the legend of Sidora may be an exception.

If you would like to know more about the legend of Sidora or if you have additional information about the legend or its mythology – or if you have other stories that you would like to share – please contact the publisher by sending an email to info@linguabooks.com. We would love to hear from you.